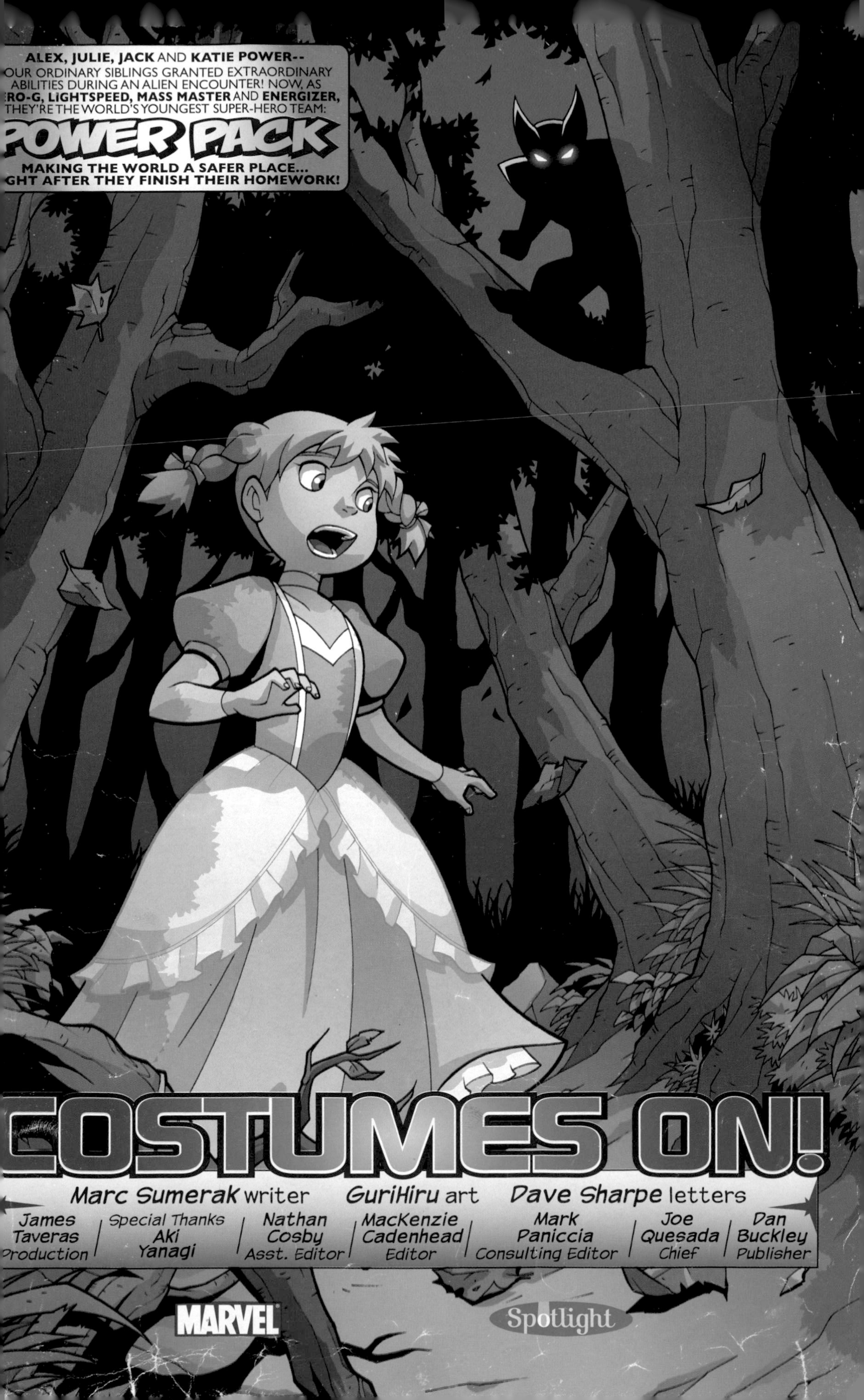

ALEX, JULIE, JACK AND KATIE POWER--
OUR ORDINARY SIBLINGS GRANTED EXTRAORDINARY
ABILITIES DURING AN ALIEN ENCOUNTER! NOW, AS
ERO-G, LIGHTSPEED, MASS MASTER AND ENERGIZER,
THEY'RE THE WORLD'S YOUNGEST SUPER-HERO TEAM:
POWER PACK
MAKING THE WORLD A SAFER PLACE...
GHT AFTER THEY FINISH THEIR HOMEWORK!
COSTUMES ON!
Marc Sumerak writer GuriHiru art Dave Sharpe letters
James Taveras Production
Special Thanks Aki Yanagi
Nathan Cosby Asst. Editor
MacKenzie Cadenhead Editor
Mark Paniccia Consulting Editor
Joe Quesada Chief
Dan Buckley Publisher
MARVEL
Spotlight

VISIT US AT
www.abdopublishing.com

Spotlight library bound edition © 2007. Spotlight is a division of ABDO Publishing Company, Edina, Minnesota.

Cataloging Data

Sumerak, Marc
    Costumes on! / Marc Sumerak, writer ; GuriHiru, art ; Dave Sharpe, letters. -- Library bound ed.
        p. cm. -- (X-Men power pack)
    Summary: Marvel's youngest superheroes Alex, Julie, Jack, and Katie team up with their idols Wolverine, Cyclops, and the other X-Men to keep the world a safer place.
    "Marvel age"--Covers.
    Revision of the December 2005 issue of Marvel age X-Men Power Pack.
    ISBN-13: 978-1-59961-220-1
    ISBN-10: 1-59961-220-8
    1. Superheroes (Fictitious characters)--Comic books, strips, etc.--Fiction.
    2. Graphic novels. I. Title. II. Series.

741.5dc22

All Spotlight books are reinforced library binding and manufactured in the United States of America

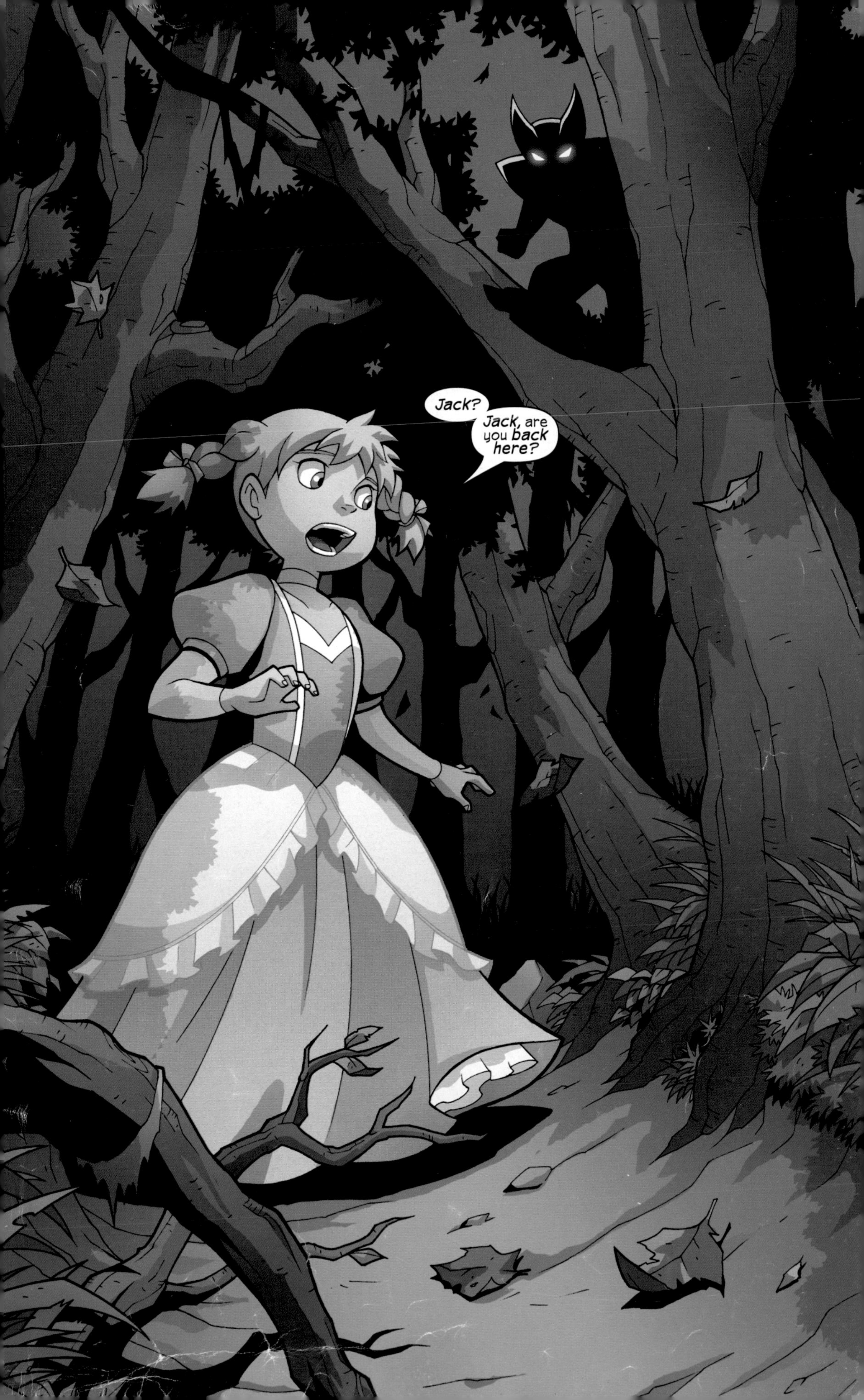
Jack?
Jack, are you back here?

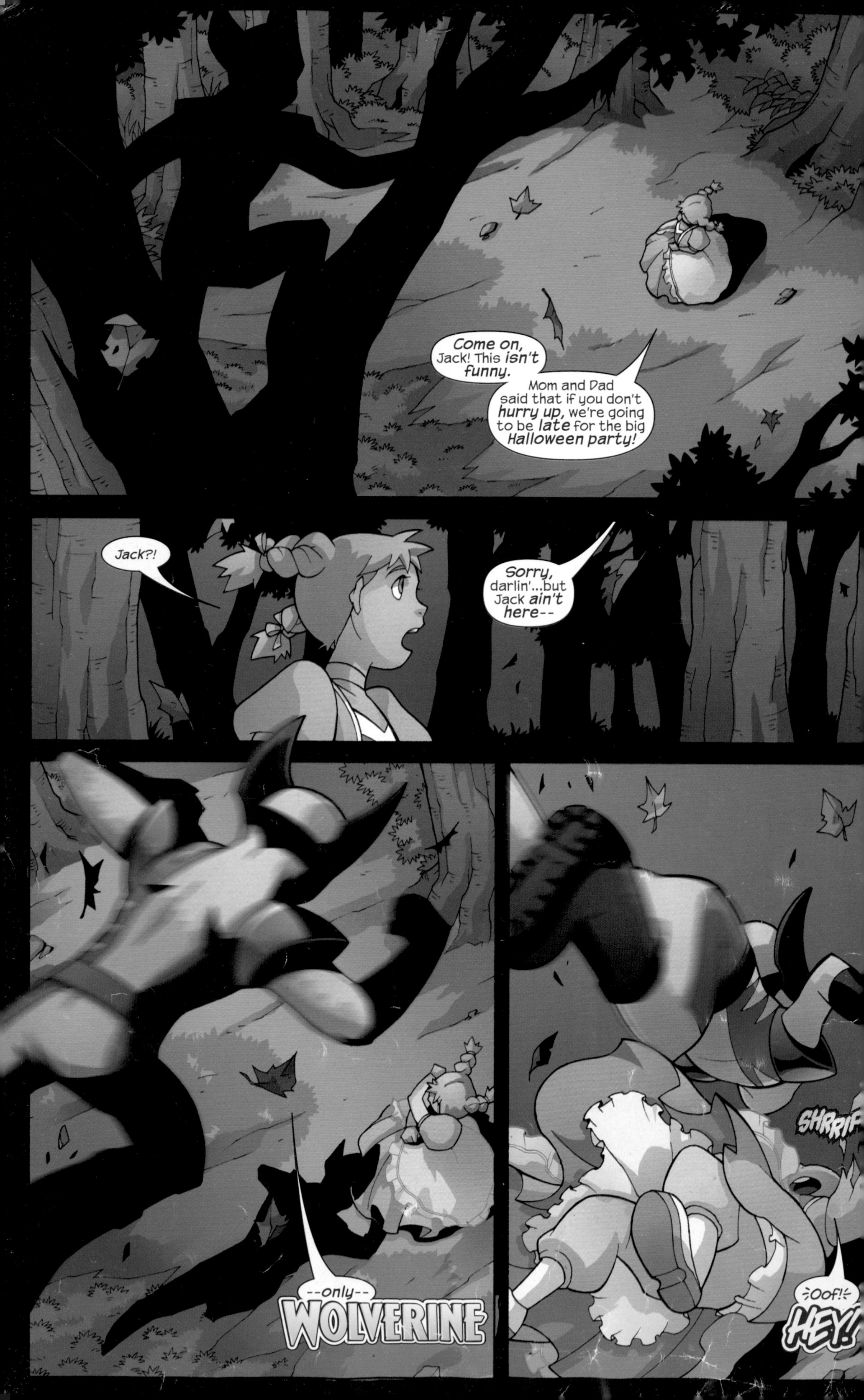
Come on, Jack! This isn't funny.
Mom and Dad said that if you don't hurry up, we're going to be late for the big Halloween party!
Jack?!
Sorry, darlin'...but Jack ain't here--
--only--
WOLVERINE
SHRRIP
Oof!
HEY!

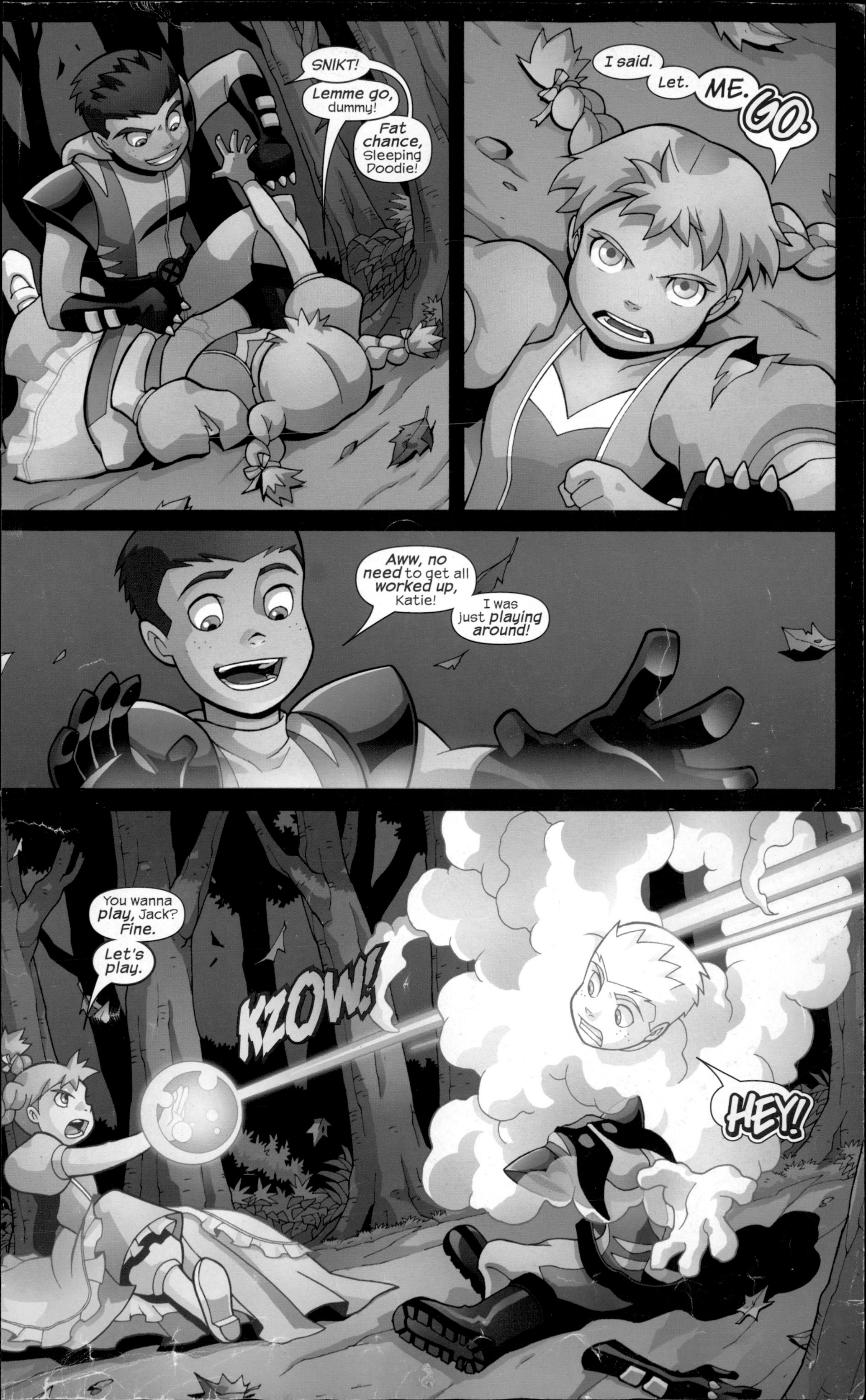
SNIKT!
Lemme go, dummy!
Fat chance, Sleeping Doodie!
I said.
Let.
ME. GO.
Aww, no need to get all worked up, Katie!
I was just playing around!
You wanna play, Jack? Fine.
Let's play.
KZOW!
HEY!

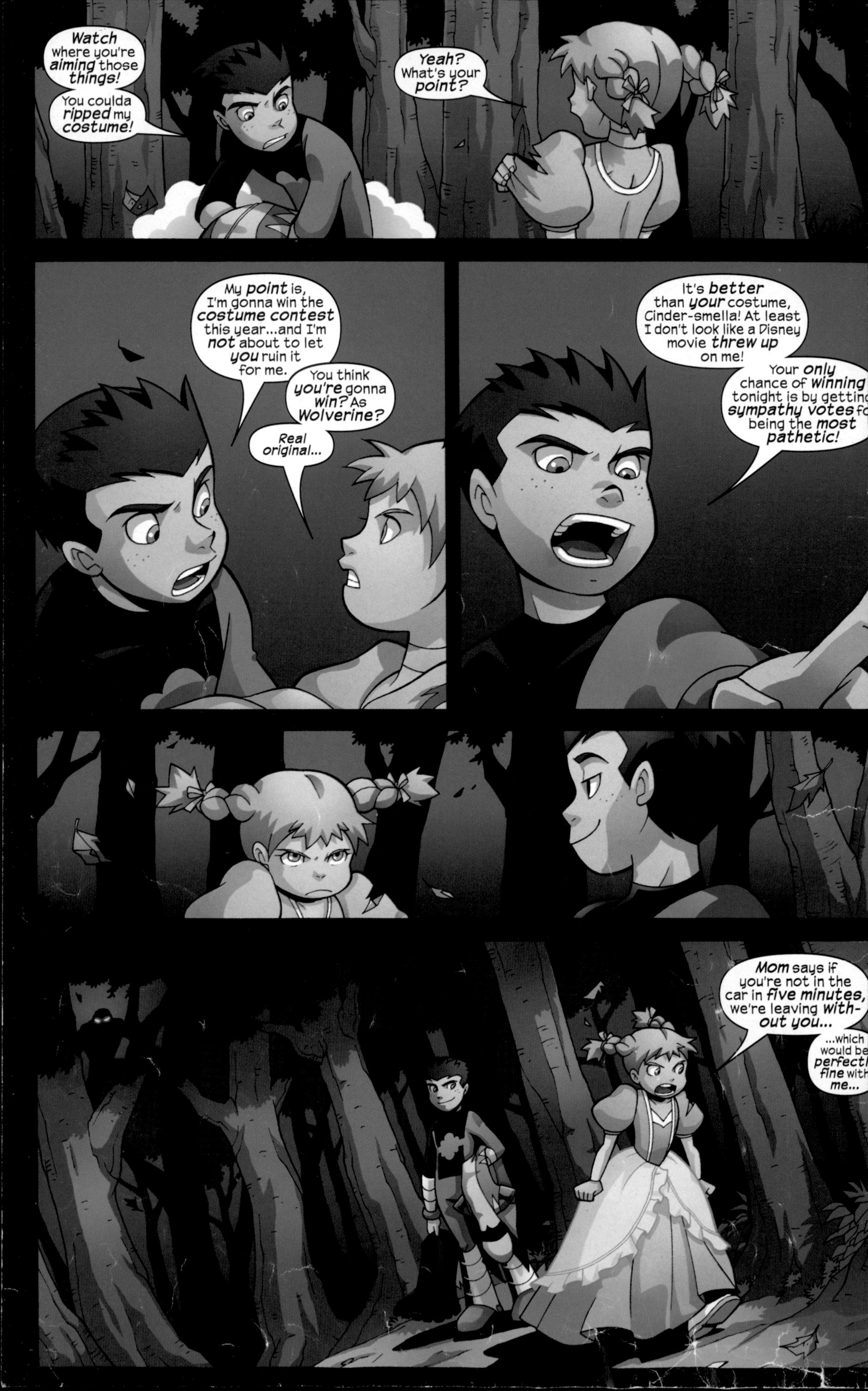
Watch where you're aiming those things!
You coulda ripped my costume!
Yeah? What's your point?
My point is, I'm gonna win the costume contest this year...and I'm not about to let you ruin it for me.
You think you're gonna win? As Wolverine?
Real original...
It's better than your costume, Cinder-smella! At least I don't look like a Disney movie threw up on me!
Your only chance of winning tonight is by getting sympathy votes for being the most pathetic!
Mom says if you're not in the car in five minutes, we're leaving with-out you...
...which would be perfectly fine with me...

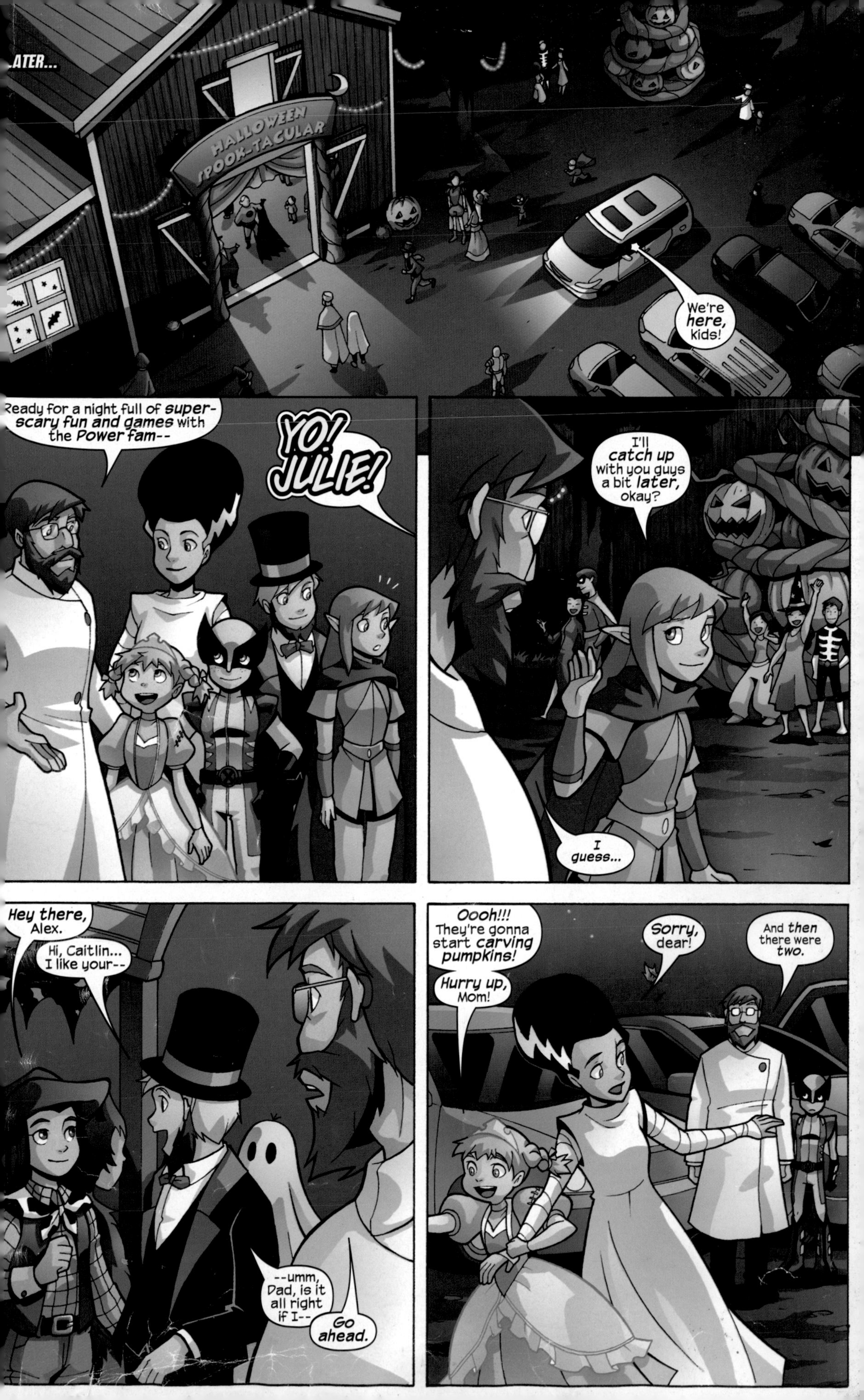
LATER...
HALLOWEEN SPOOK-TACULAR
We're here, kids!
Ready for a night full of super-scary fun and games with the Power fam--
YO! JULIE!
I'll catch up with you guys a bit later, okay?
I guess...
Hey there, Alex.
Hi, Caitlin... I like your--
--umm, Dad, is it all right if I--
Go ahead.
Oooh!!! They're gonna start carving pumpkins!
Hurry up, Mom!
Sorry, dear!
And then there were two.

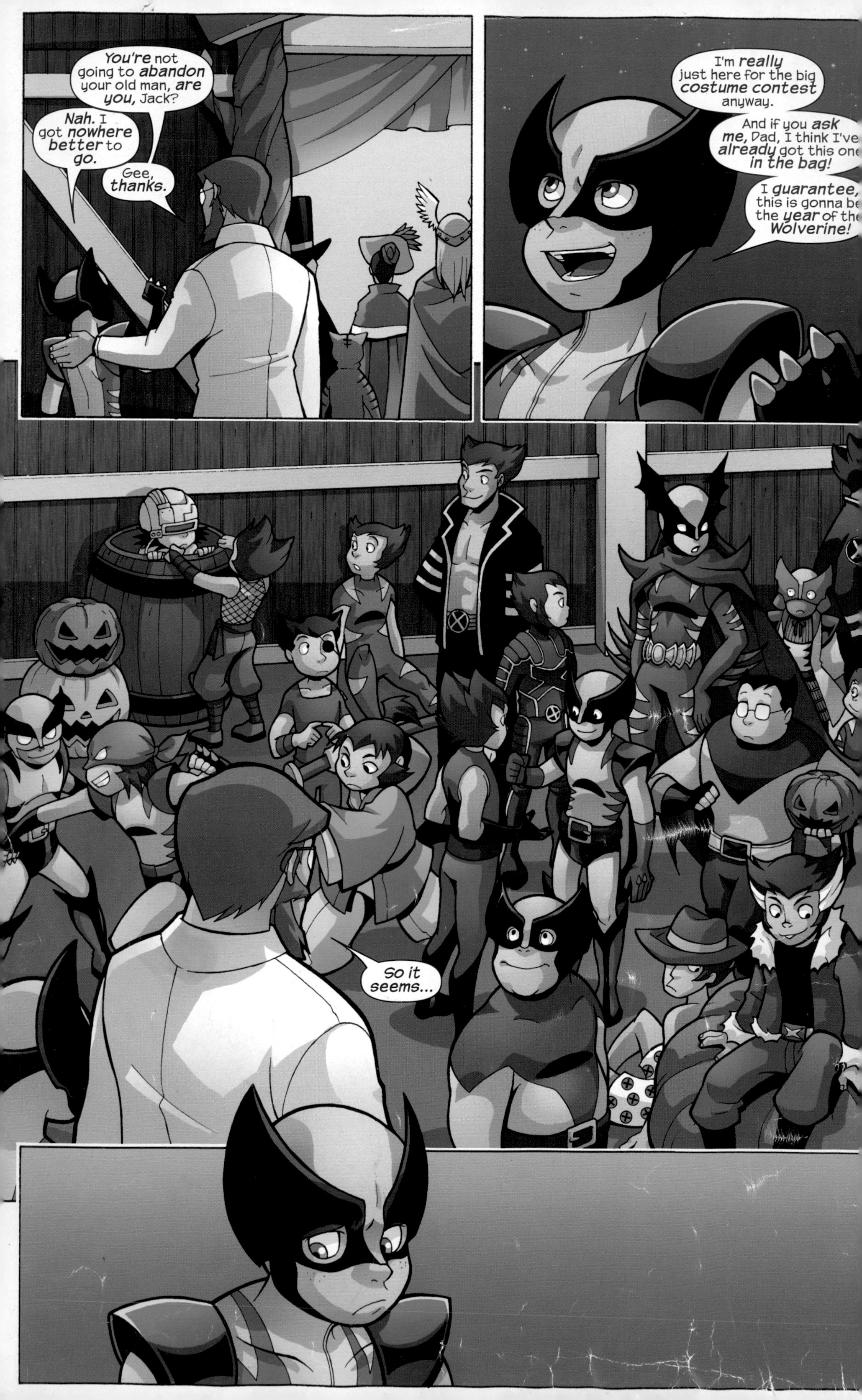
You're not going to abandon your old man, are you, Jack?
Nah. I got nowhere better to go.
Gee, thanks.
I'm really just here for the big costume contest anyway.
And if you ask me, Dad, I think I've already got this one in the bag!
I guarantee, this is gonna be the year of the Wolverine!
So it seems...

Way to go, Katie!

Great bobbing!

...stupid Halloween party...

Jack?

Hey...you *okay?*

No.

Does it *look* like I *am?*

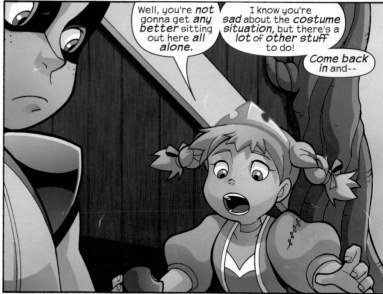

Well, you're *not* gonna get *any better* sitting out here all *alone.*

I know you're *sad* about the *costume situation,* but there's a *lot* of *other stuff* to do!

Come back in and--

And *what?*

Play *dumb party games* with *you* and the *rest* of the *rugrats?*

Thanks, but *I'll skip.*

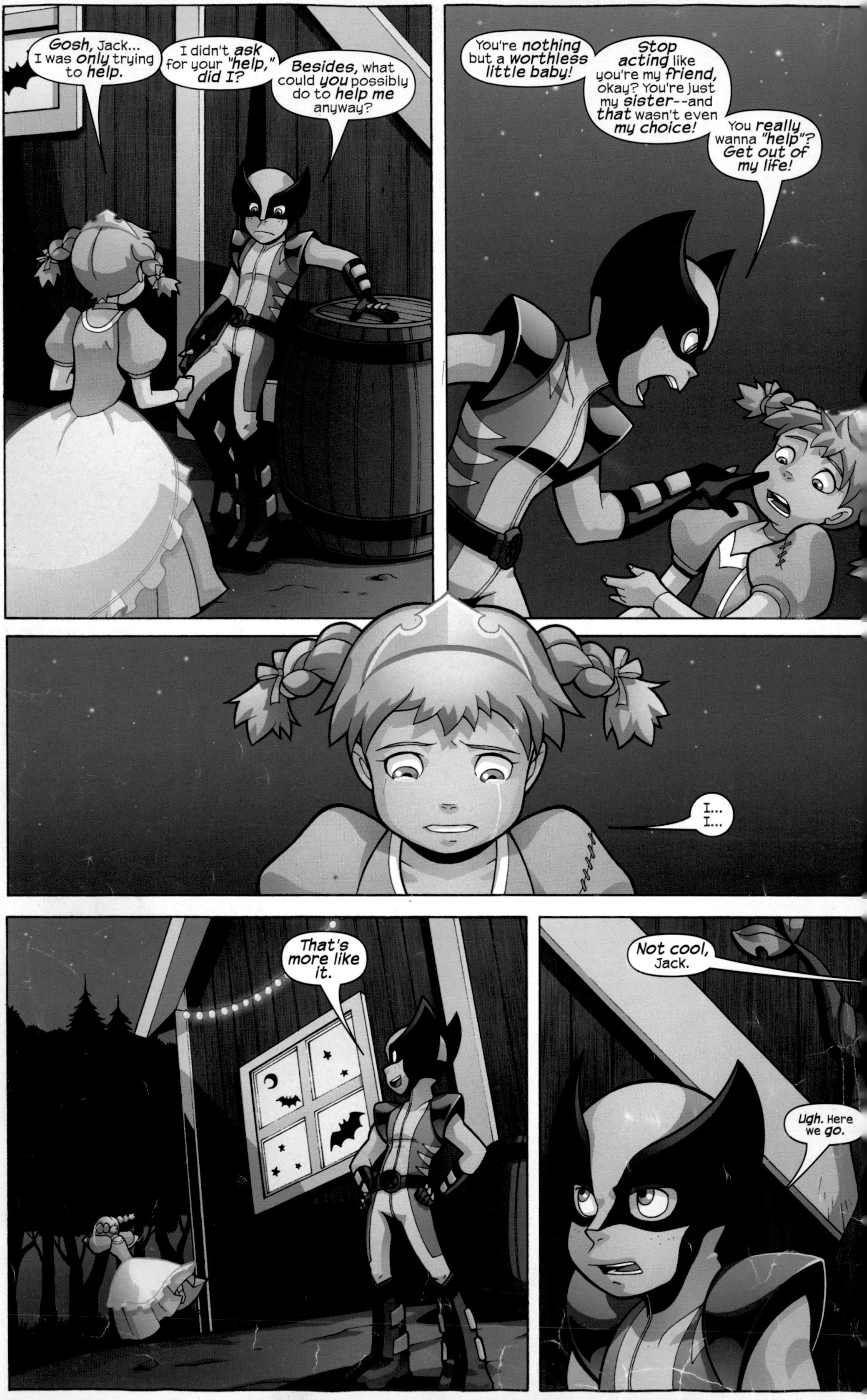
Gosh, Jack... I was only trying to help.
I didn't ask for your "help," did I?
Besides, what could you possibly do to help me anyway?
You're nothing but a worthless little baby!
Stop acting like you're my friend, okay? You're just my sister--and that wasn't even my choice!
You really wanna "help"? Get out of my life!
I... I...
That's more like it.
Not cool, Jack.
Ugh. Here we go.

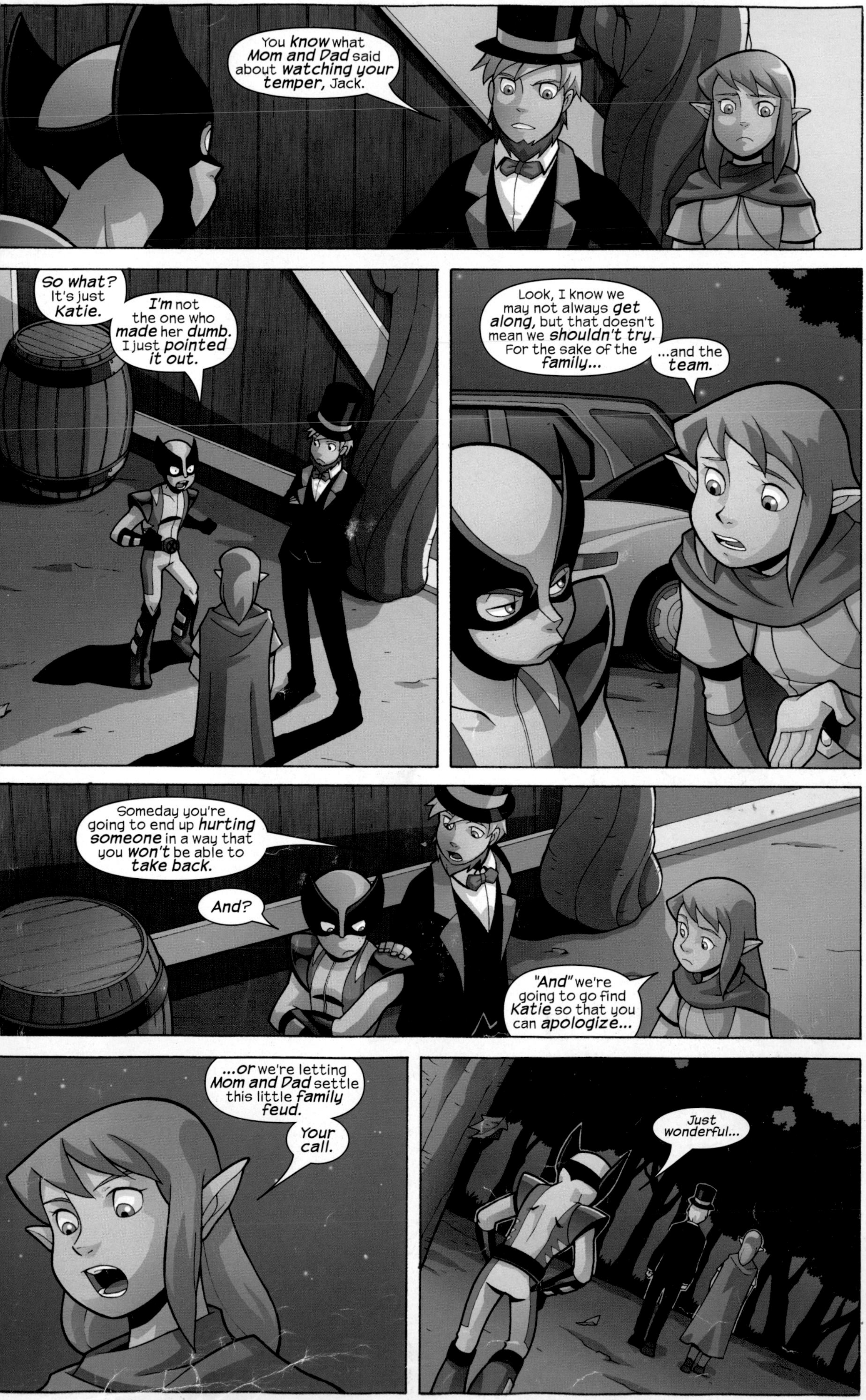
You know what Mom and Dad said about watching your temper, Jack.
So what? It's just Katie.
I'm not the one who made her dumb. I just pointed it out.
Look, I know we may not always get along, but that doesn't mean we shouldn't try. For the sake of the family...
...and the team.
Someday you're going to end up hurting someone in a way that you won't be able to take back.
And?
"And" we're going to go find Katie so that you can apologize...
...or we're letting Mom and Dad settle this little family feud.
Your call.
Just wonderful...

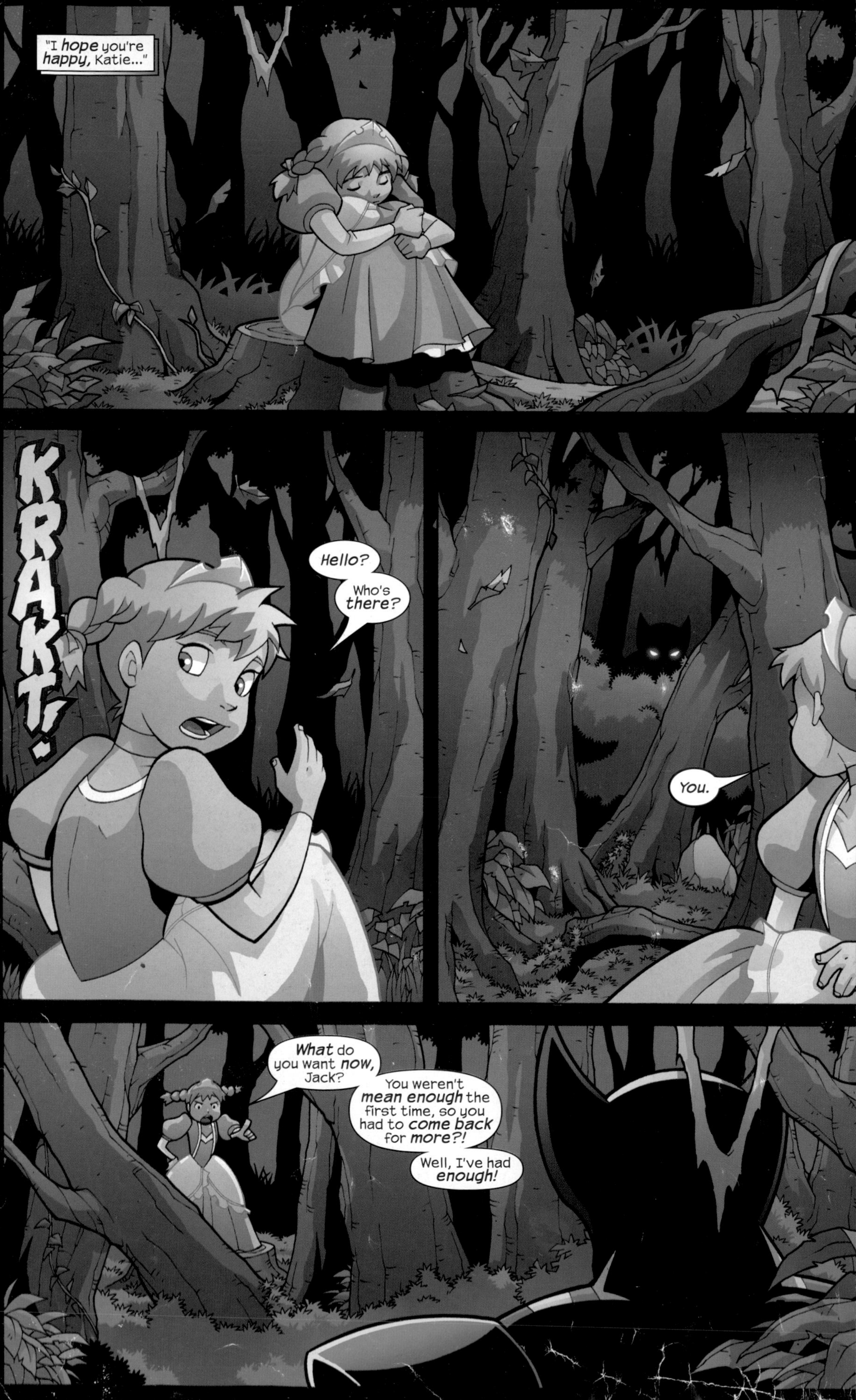
"I hope you're happy, Katie..."
KRAKT!
Hello?
Who's there?
You.
What do you want now, Jack?
You weren't mean enough the first time, so you had to come back for more?!
Well, I've had enough!

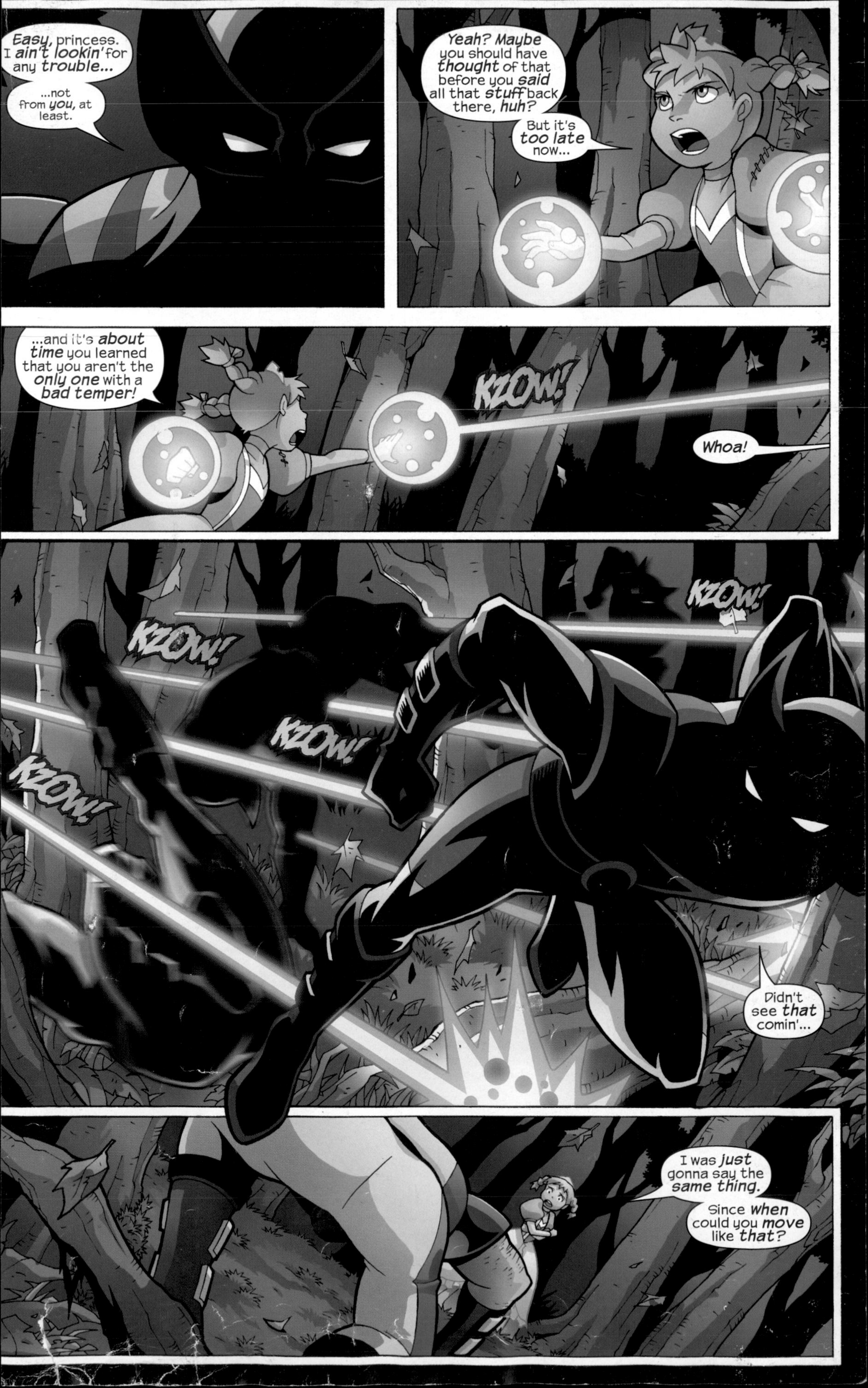

Easy, princess. I ain't lookin' for any trouble...
...not from you, at least.
Yeah? Maybe you should have thought of that before you said all that stuff back there, huh?
But it's too late now...
...and it's about time you learned that you aren't the only one with a bad temper!
KZOW!
Whoa!
KZOW!
KZOW!
KZOW!
KZOW!
Didn't see that comin'...
I was just gonna say the same thing.
Since when could you move like that?

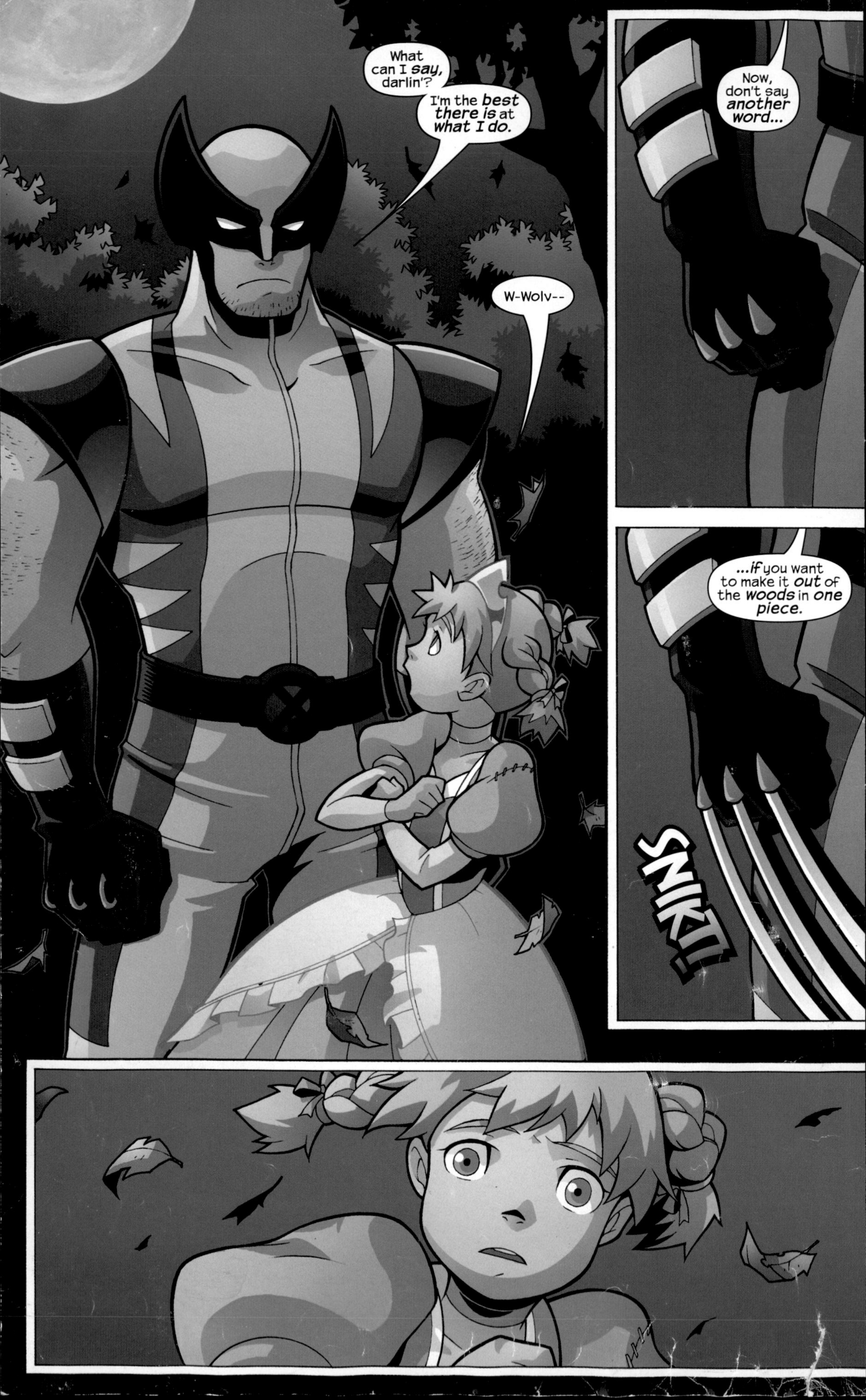
What can I say, darlin'?
I'm the best there is at what I do.
W-Wolv--
Now, don't say another word...
...if you want to make it out of the woods in one piece.
SNIKT!

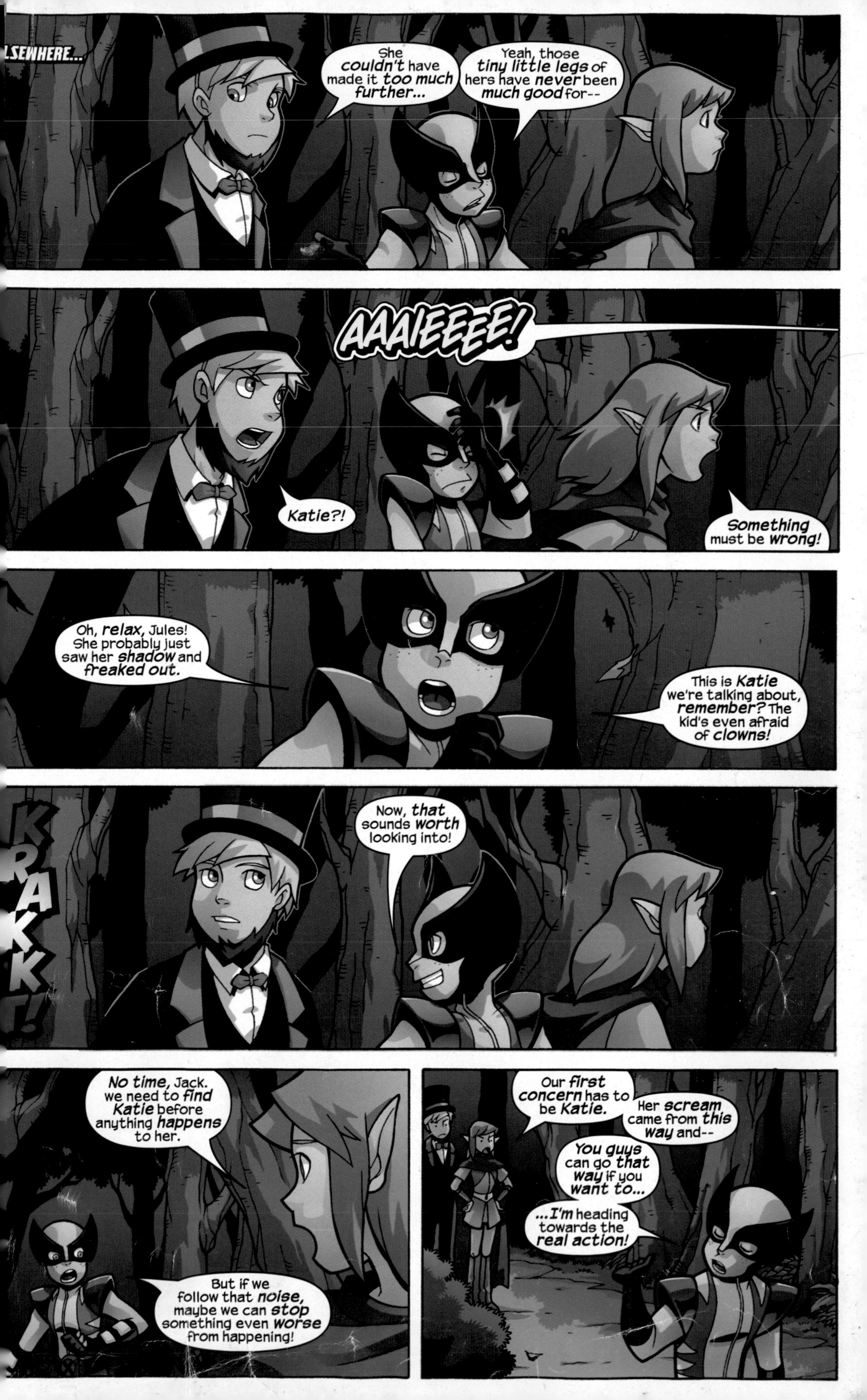
ELSEWHERE...
She couldn't have made it too much further...
Yeah, those tiny little legs of hers have never been much good for--
AAAIEEEEE!
Katie?!
Something must be wrong!
Oh, relax, Jules! She probably just saw her shadow and freaked out.
This is Katie we're talking about, remember? The kid's even afraid of clowns!
KRAKK!
Now, that sounds worth looking into!
No time, Jack. we need to find Katie before anything happens to her.
But if we follow that noise, maybe we can stop something even worse from happening!
Our first concern has to be Katie.
Her scream came from this way and--
You guys can go that way if you want to...
...I'm heading towards the real action!

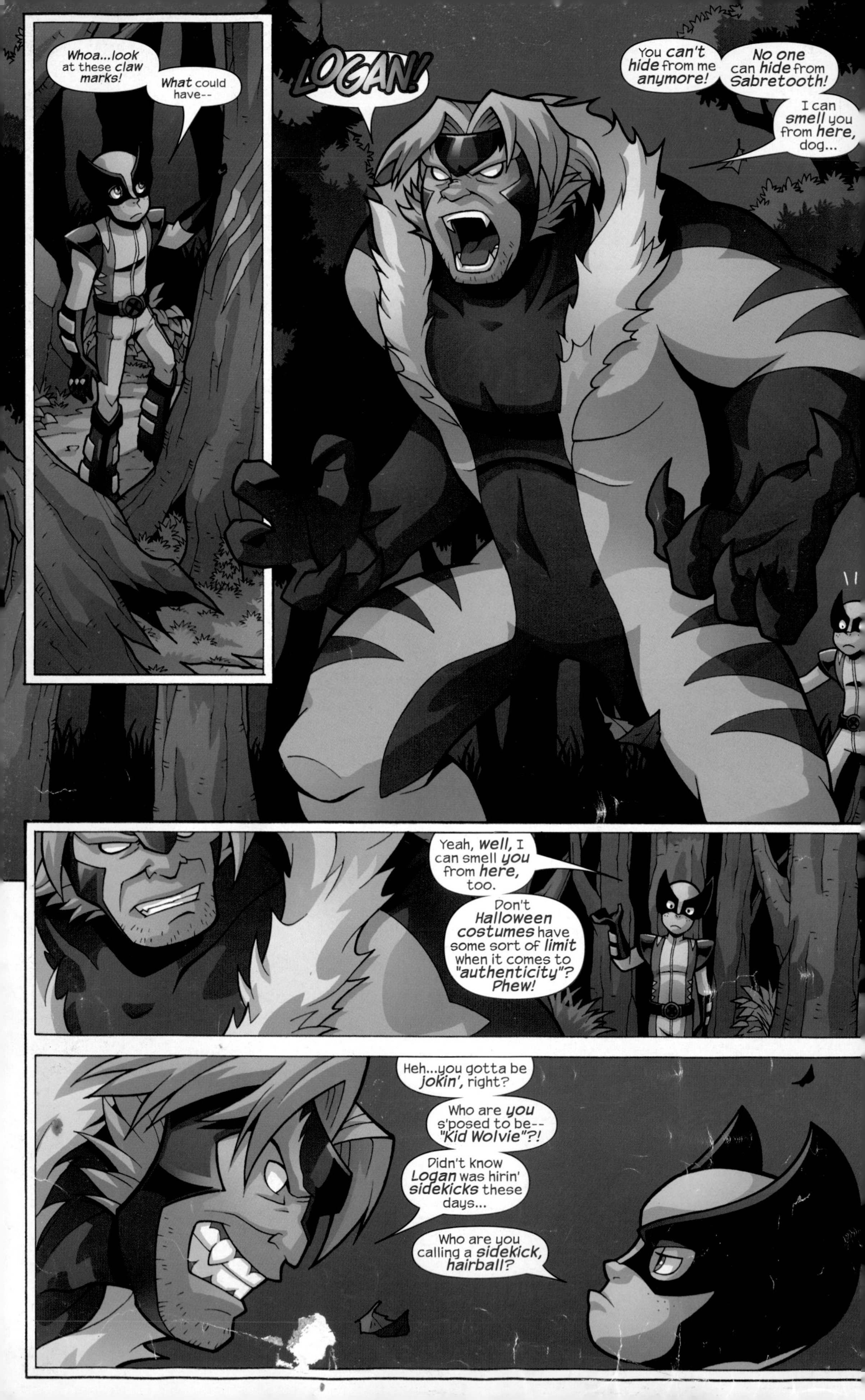

Whoa...look at these claw marks!
What could have--
LOGAN!
You can't hide from me anymore!
No one can hide from Sabretooth!
I can smell you from here, dog...
Yeah, well, I can smell you from here, too.
Don't Halloween costumes have some sort of limit when it comes to "authenticity"? Phew!
Heh...you gotta be jokin', right?
Who are you s'posed to be-- "Kid Wolvie"?!
Didn't know Logan was hirin' sidekicks these days...
Who are you calling a sidekick, hairball?

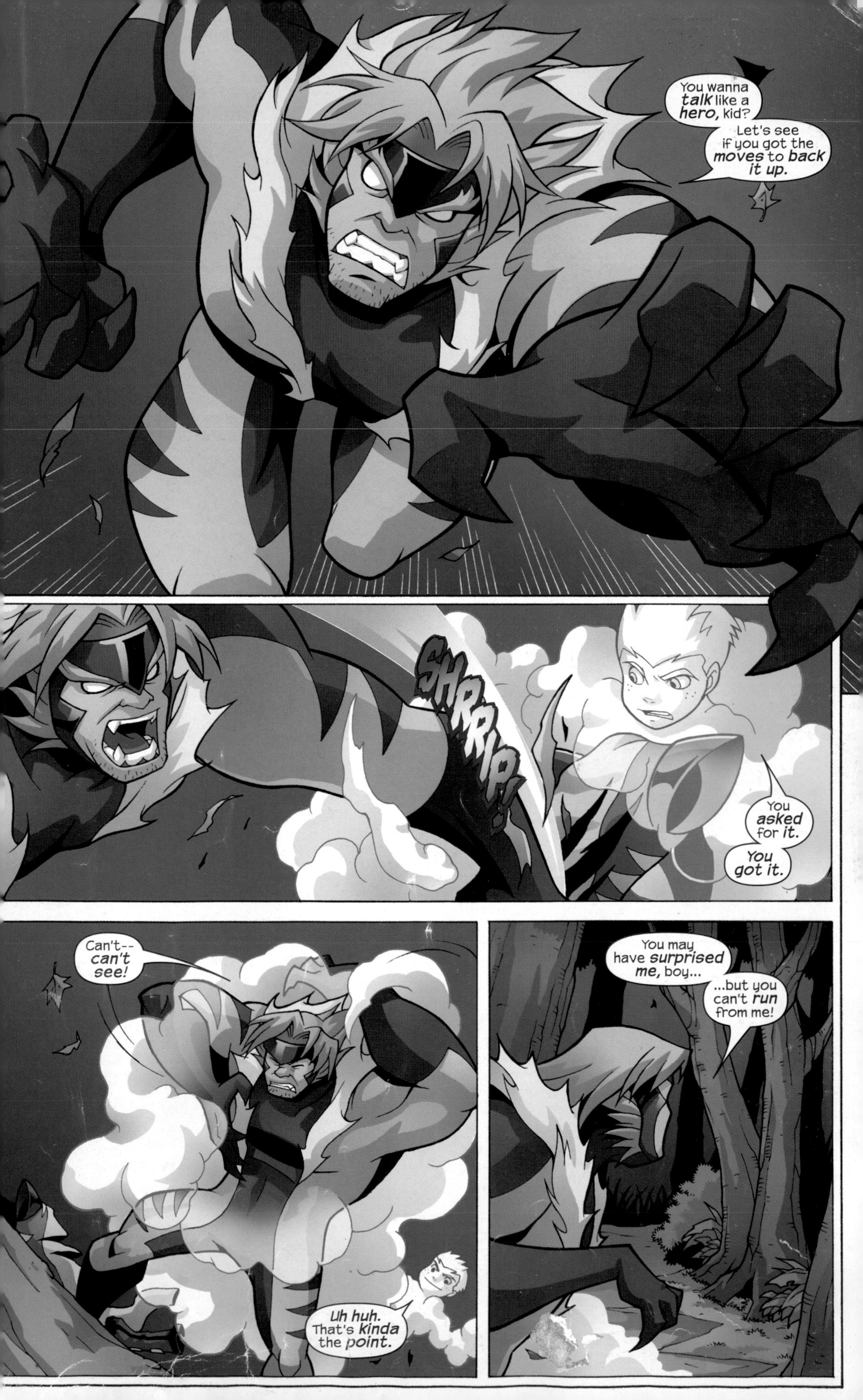
You wanna *talk* like a *hero,* kid?
Let's see if you got the *moves* to *back it up.*
SHRRIP!
You *asked* for *it.*
You got it.
Can't-- *can't see!*
Uh huh. That's *kinda* the *point.*
You may have *surprised me,* boy...
...but you can't *run* from me!

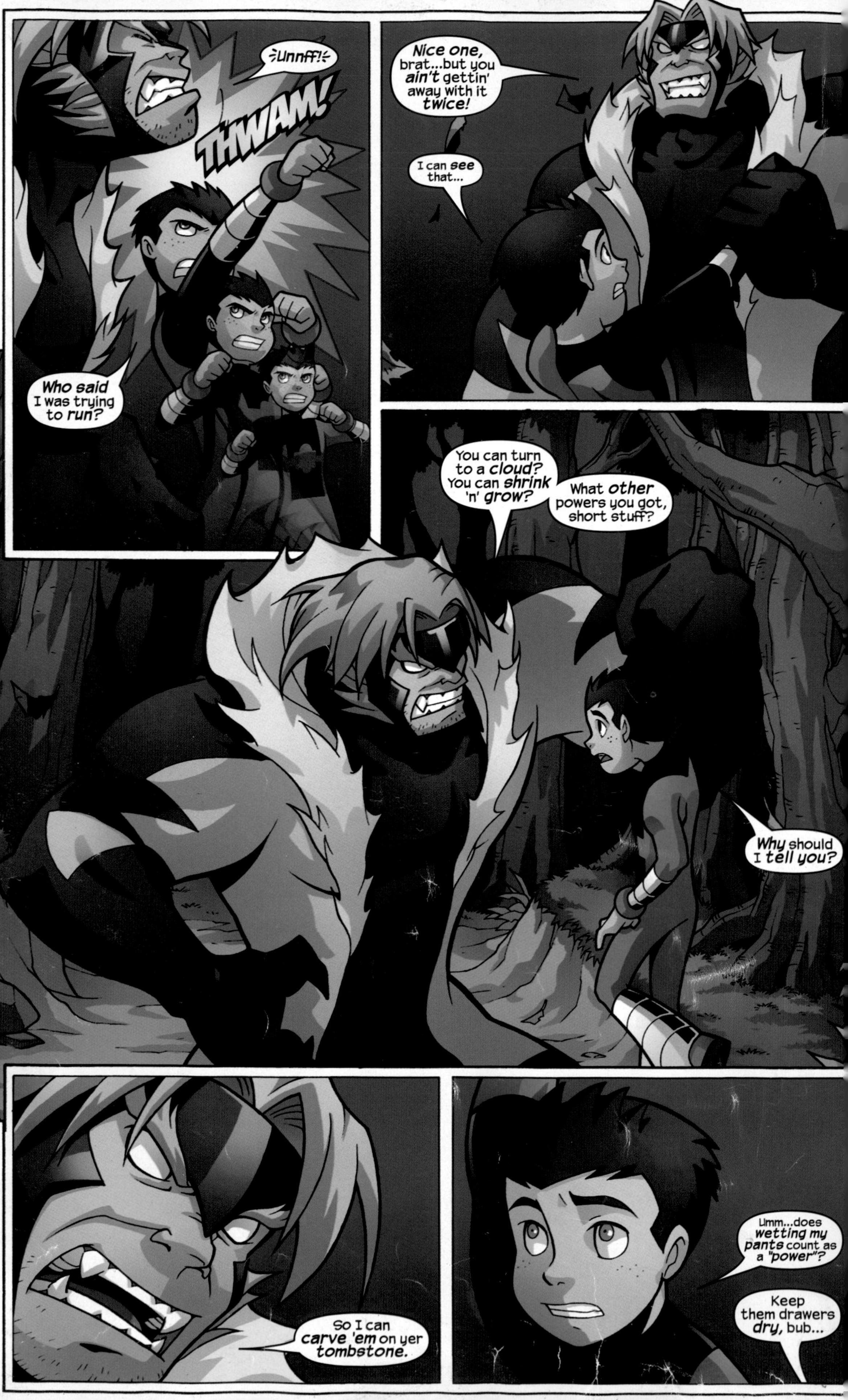

Unnff!
THWAM!
Who said I was trying to run?
Nice one, brat...but you ain't gettin' away with it twice!
I can see that...
You can turn to a cloud? You can shrink 'n' grow?
What other powers you got, short stuff?
Why should I tell you?
So I can carve 'em on yer tombstone.
Umm...does wetting my pants count as a "power"?
Keep them drawers dry, bub...

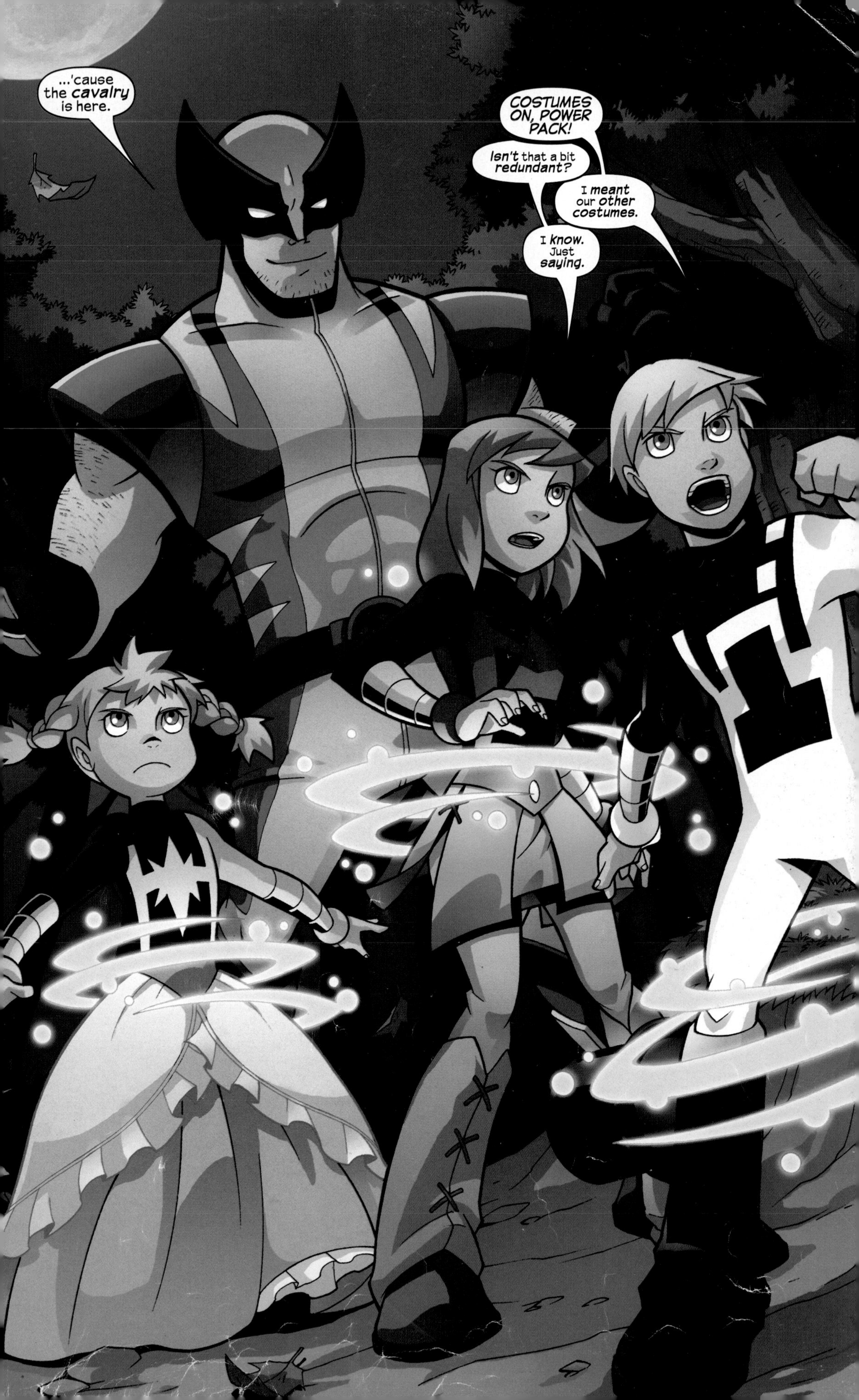
...'cause the cavalry is here.
COSTUMES ON, POWER PACK!
Isn't that a bit redundant?
I meant our other costumes.
I know. Just saying.

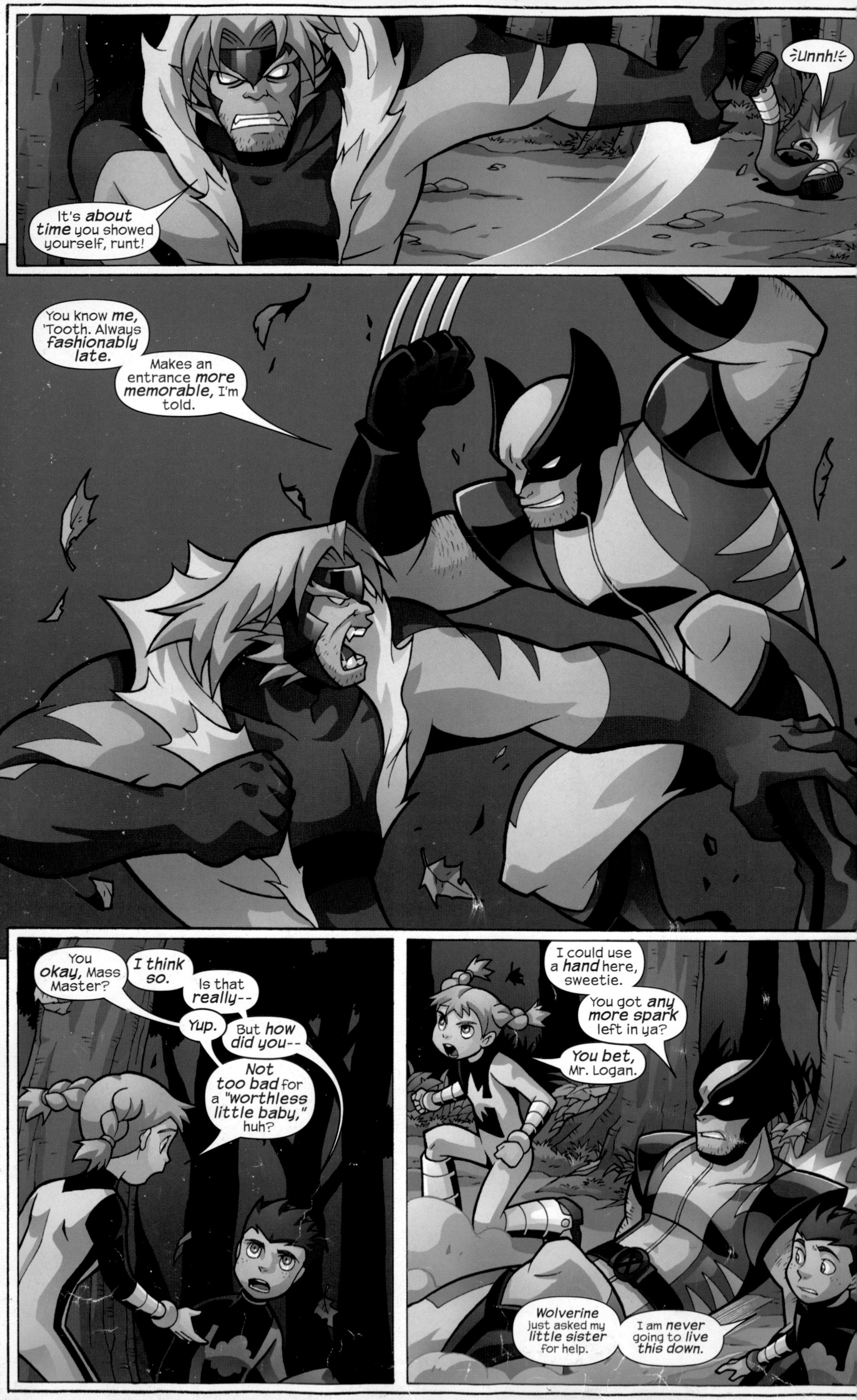

It's about time you showed yourself, runt!
Unnh!
You know me, 'Tooth. Always fashionably late.
Makes an entrance more memorable, I'm told.
You okay, Mass Master?
I think so.
Is that really--
Yup.
But how did you--
Not too bad for a "worthless little baby," huh?
I could use a hand here, sweetie.
You got any more spark left in ya?
You bet, Mr. Logan.
Wolverine just asked my little sister for help.
I am never going to live this down.

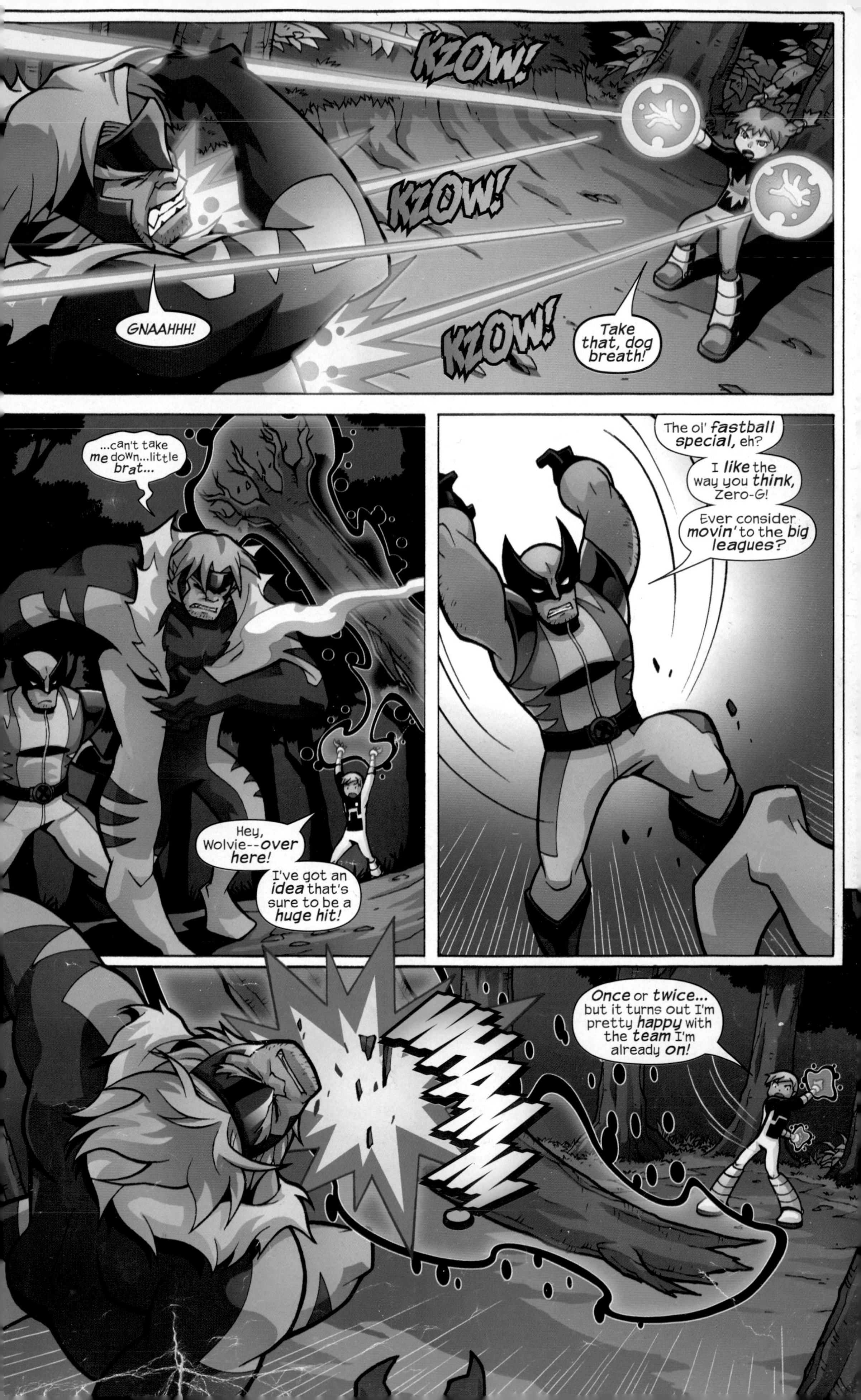
KZOW!
KZOW!
GNAAHHH!
KZOW!
Take that, dog breath!
...can't take me down...little brat...
Hey, Wolvie--over here!
I've got an idea that's sure to be a huge hit!
The ol' fastball special, eh?
I like the way you think, Zero-G!
Ever consider movin' to the big leagues?
WHAMM!
Once or twice... but it turns out I'm pretty happy with the team I'm already on!

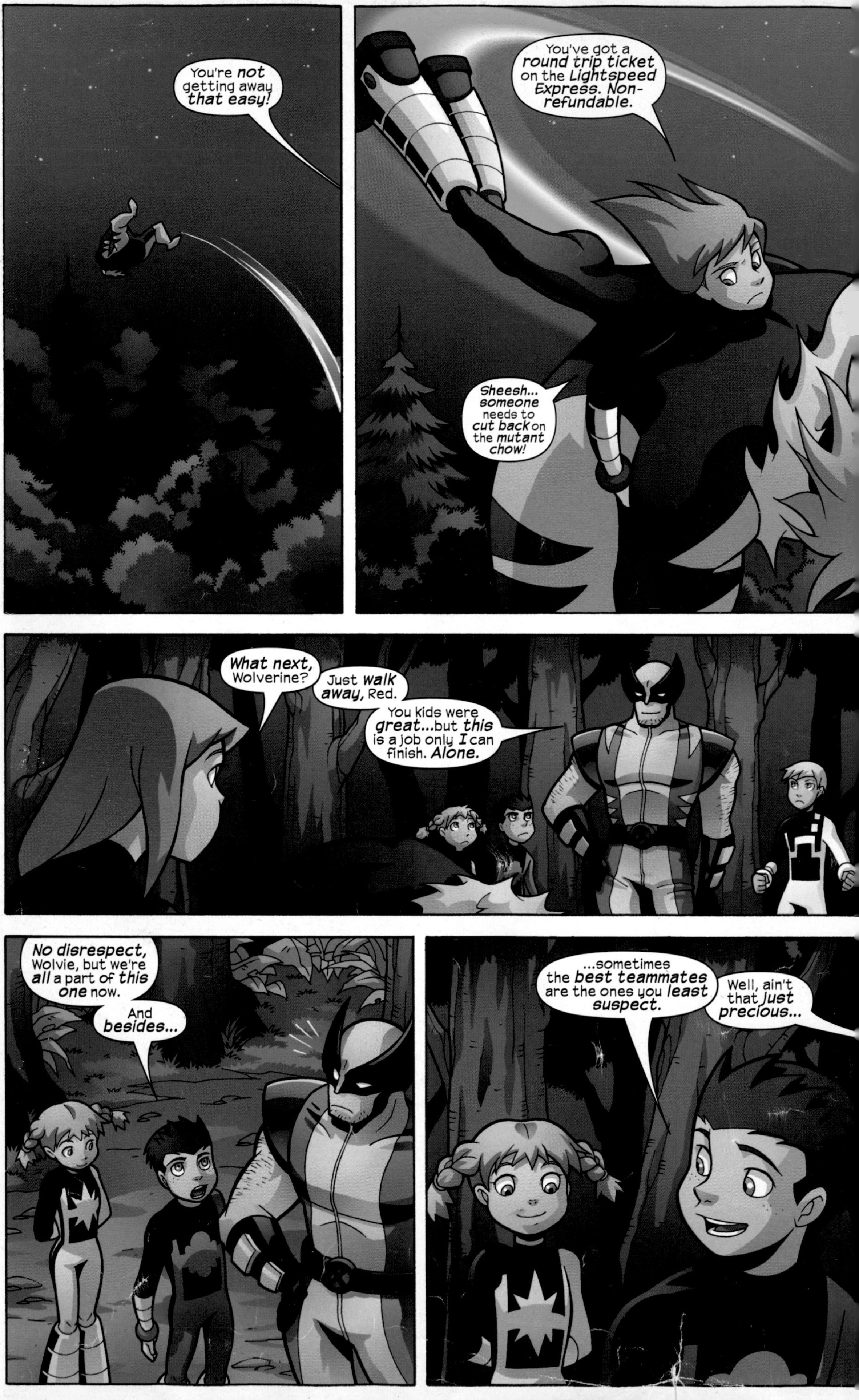

You're not getting away that easy!
You've got a round trip ticket on the Lightspeed Express. Non-refundable.
Sheesh... someone needs to cut back on the mutant chow!
What next, Wolverine?
Just walk away, Red.
You kids were great...but this is a job only I can finish. Alone.
No disrespect, Wolvie, but we're all a part of this one now.
And besides...
...sometimes the best teammates are the ones you least suspect.
Well, ain't that just precious...

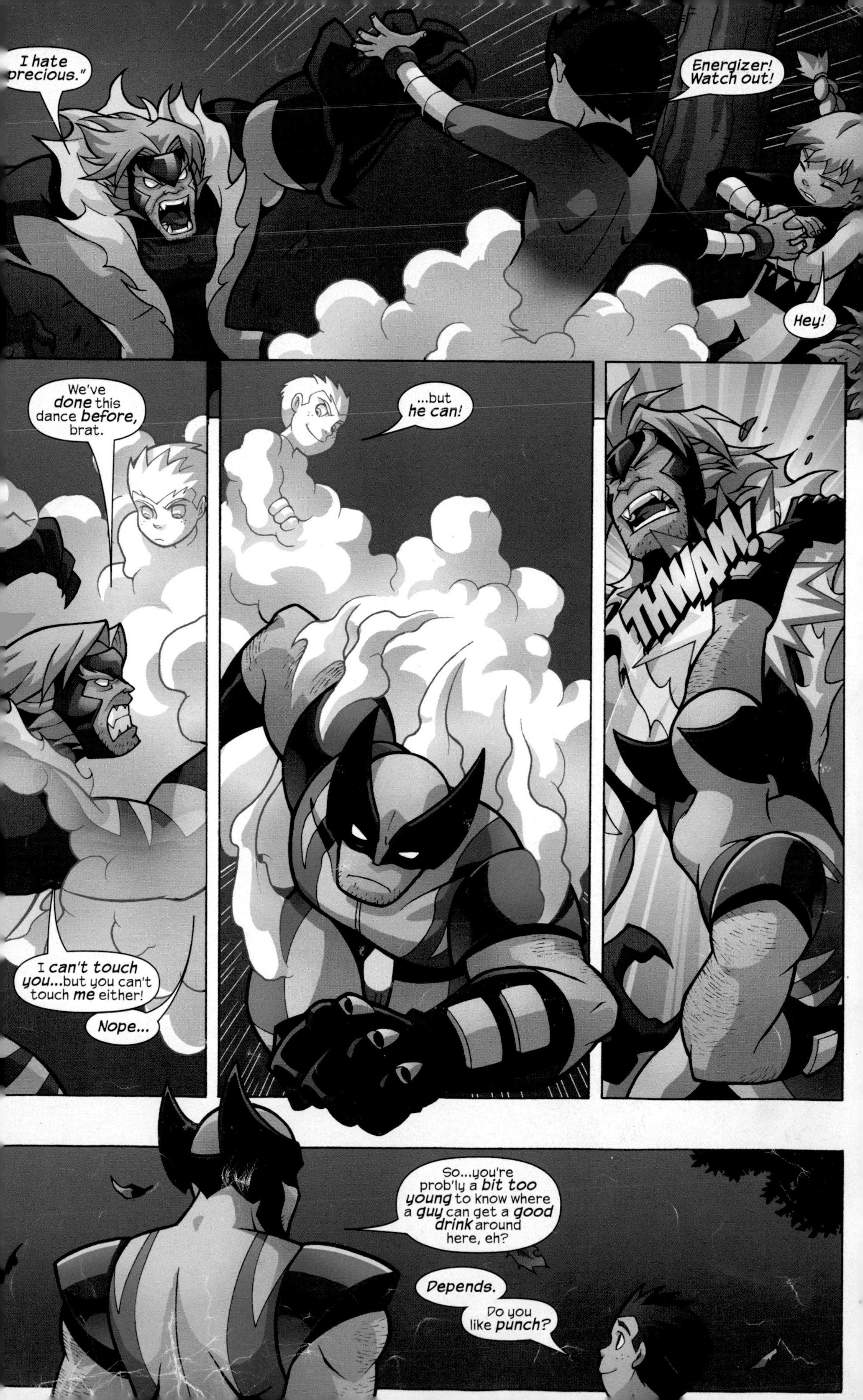
I hate precious."
Energizer! Watch out!
Hey!
We've done this dance before, brat.
I can't touch you...but you can't touch me either!
Nope...
...but he can!
THWAM!
So...you're prob'ly a bit too young to know where a guy can get a good drink around here, eh?
Depends.
Do you like punch?

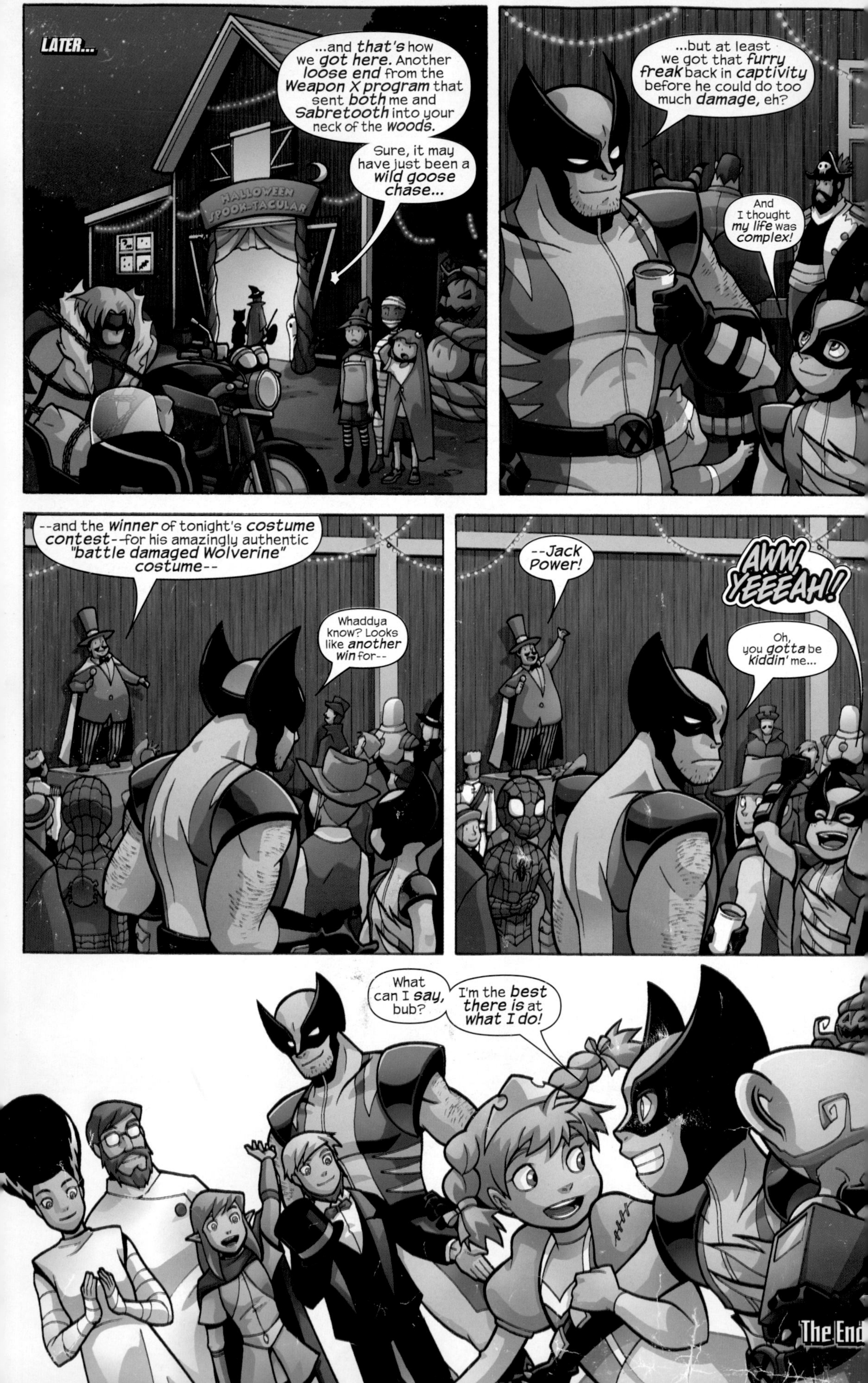
LATER...
...and that's how we got here. Another loose end from the Weapon X program that sent both me and Sabretooth into your neck of the woods.
Sure, it may have just been a wild goose chase...
HALLOWEEN SPOOK-TACULAR
...but at least we got that furry freak back in captivity before he could do too much damage, eh?
And I thought my life was complex!
--and the winner of tonight's costume contest--for his amazingly authentic "battle damaged Wolverine" costume--
Whaddya know? Looks like another win for--
--Jack Power!
AWW YEEEAH!!
Oh, you gotta be kiddin' me...
What can I say, bub?
I'm the best there is at what I do!
The End